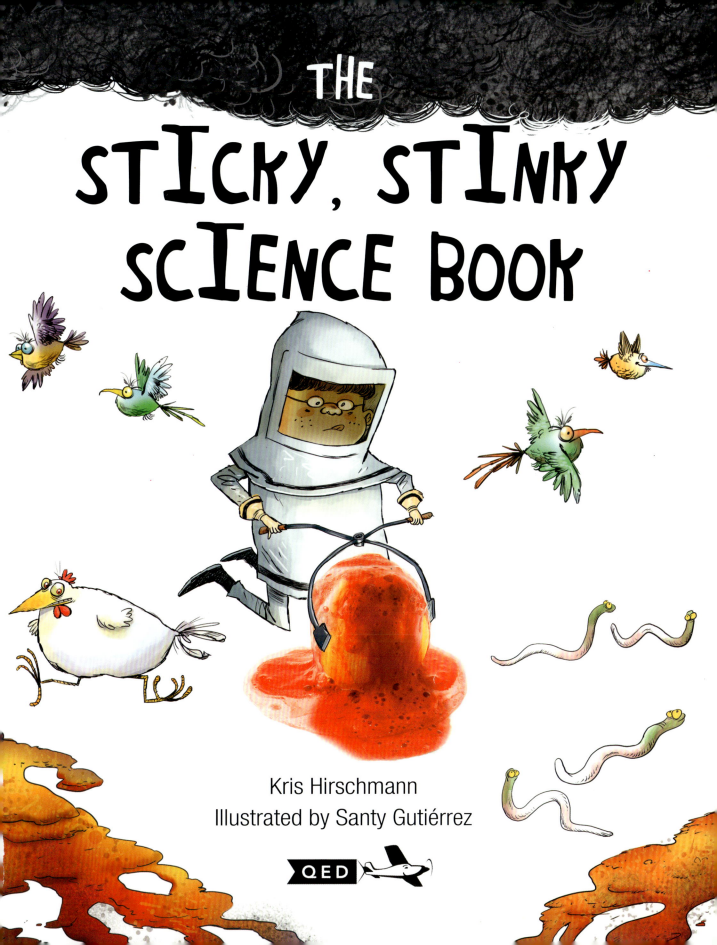

Quarto is the authority on a wide range of topics.

Quarto educates, entertains and enriches the lives of our readers—enthusiasts and lovers of hands-on living.

www.quartoknows.com

This edition first published in 2018
by QED Publishing,
an imprint of The Quarto Group.
The Old Brewery, 6 Blundell Street,
London N7 9BH, United Kingdom.
T (0)20 7700 6700 F (0)20 7700 8066
www.QuartoKnows.com

A catalogue record for this book is available from the British Library.

ISBN 978 1 91241 367 6

Manufactured in Guangdong, China CC062018

9 8 7 6 5 4 3 2 1

Editor: Harriet Stone
Designer: Kevin Knight
Editorial Director: Laura Knowles
Art Director: Susi Martin
Publisher: Maxime Boucknooghe
Production: Nikki Ingram

Acknowledgements

The publisher would like to thank the following agencies for their kind permission to use their images.

Picture Credits

(t=top, b=bottom, l=left, r=right, c=centre)

Alamy

9c Simon Perkin (Commercial), 13tr PJF Military Collection, 23c Science Photo Library, 46l Dragan Zivkovic, 49br Carolyn Jenkins, 53l Ikon Images

Shutterstock

3br Yulia Glam, 8tl Kevin Tavares, 16tl Anneka, 16bl Eric Isselee, 19tr wildestanimal, 25bl Jorge Salcedo, 26tl Samet Guler, 26bl Piotr Wawrzyniuk, 29tl Sylvia Kania, 29br fboudrias, 32tr Daniela Pelazza, 36c trgrowth, 38tl Satirus, 38tr nexus 7, 38c 3445128471, 38bc Basileus, 39l Africa Studio, 43tr KaliAntye, 43br sarocha wangdee, 46b Iakov Filimonov, 47br MikeBraune, 49tr Tony Thiethoaly, 50bl Anton Prado PHOTO, 52tr TroobaDoor, 52b CKP1001, 54r Alexander Lobanov, 54l f/stop, 54c Winston Link, 57tl Holly Kuchera, 58-59bc serenarossi, 61r Andrea Izzotti, 61b Jose Ignacio Soto

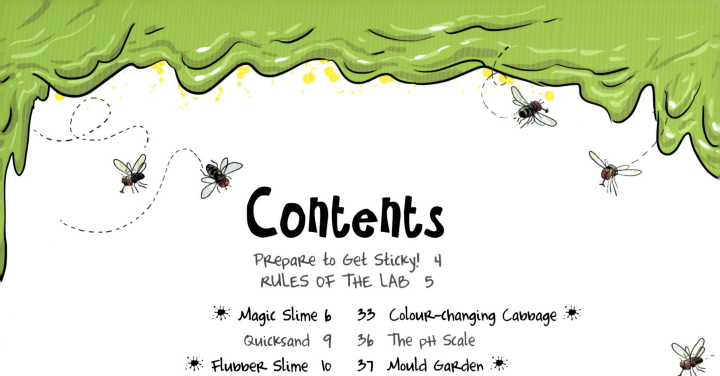

Contents

Prepare to Get Sticky! 4
RULES OF THE LAB 5

✳ = Science experiment

Prepare to Get Sticky!

When you think of scientists at work, do you picture a sparkling laboratory? White coats? Sterile conditions? Clean, clean, clean? Well, science isn't always like that.

In this book, science gets down and dirty. You're about to dive into a world where things are STICKY; where they're STINKY; where they're just plain messy, yucky and disgusting. In other words, where science is much more fun than you'd think!

But guess what? Here's the really cool part: IT'S STILL SCIENCE. Which means that besides doing some amazing stuff, you're also going to learn a few things. You'll find out why slime is slimy, why plants rot into gooey puddles, why some things smell really bad, and much more. It's going to be an epic journey of yucky discovery.

So, are you ready to make a mess? We thought so! Read the lab rules on the next page, then dive right in. Oh, and one last thing: you might want to hold your nose, we're just warning you…

RULES OF THE LAB

Please help with my experiment

RULE 1

Always ask an adult for permission before doing the experiments in this book. Get an adult to help if the instructions tell you to. NO CHEATING on this one.

RULE 2

Be tidy! (Yes, we know the experiments are messy, but do your best.) Work on a clean, flat surface, near a sink whenever possible. Cover your work area with newspaper before starting.

RULE 3

Don't put slime or other sticky concoctions down the sink. Put them in the bin.

RULE 4

Clean up after yourself when you've finished experimenting.

RULE 5

Wash your hands!

Check out the science lingo on p63 for definitions of technical terms.

Magic Slime

It's a liquid! Oh no, sorry, it's a solid. HOLD ON – now it's a liquid again! What is going on here?? It's not really magic, it's just a little weird science to brighten up your day. A simple slime called oobleck has been delighting kids and adults for decades. Now it's your turn to plunge your hands into this ooey, gooey, liquid-but-solid-but-liquid gloop.

WHAT YOU'LL NEED

- cornflour
- water
- food colouring
- small drinking cup
- mixing bowl
- stirring spoon

Making magic slime

1 Fill the drinking cup to the brim with cornflour. Put it into the mixing bowl. Repeat to add another cup of cornflour.

2 Fill the same cup with water. Add several drops of food colouring (whatever colour you like).

3 Pour the coloured water into the bowl.

4 Now comes the fun part! Use your stirring spoon to mix the cornflour and water. At first it will be easy to stir the mixture. As the ingredients start to blend it will get harder and harder. Stir slowly for best results.

5 If the gloop is too thick to stir, add a little bit of water. If it's too runny, add a little bit of cornflour.

6 Your magic slime is ready when it forms a smooth, thick gloop that you can stir slowly, but which seizes up if you stir quickly.

Gloop!

Play with your magic slime

Now you've made your oobleck, it's time for the fun! Err, wait... I mean, it's time for some super-serious scientific observation.

1 Plunge your hand right into the slime. That's right, go on! Pull out a fistful of the stuff.

2 Roll the slime between your palms. It will form a solid ball.

3 Now stop rolling. The slime melts into goo!

4 Roll the slime into a ball again. Very quickly pull the ball apart. The slime R-R-RIPS like paper.

5 LOOK NOW! The two parts of the ball are melting into liquid again!

Weird!

The sticky, stinky science

Magic slime, or oobleck, acts the way it does because of the shape of the cornflour molecules. They are branched, like little bushes. When you put pressure on the slime, the molecules squish together and get all tangled up. They trap the water between their branches. Nothing can move, so the substance acts like a solid. When you release the pressure, the molecules separate, and the slime can move again.

WHAT'S GOING TO HAPPEN?

Put a small toy animal on the magic slime in the bowl. What happens? Will it sit on top or sink under?

STICKY TIP!

Keep your magic slime in the fridge for more experimenting later. Add a little water to re-gloopify it, if it starts to dry out.

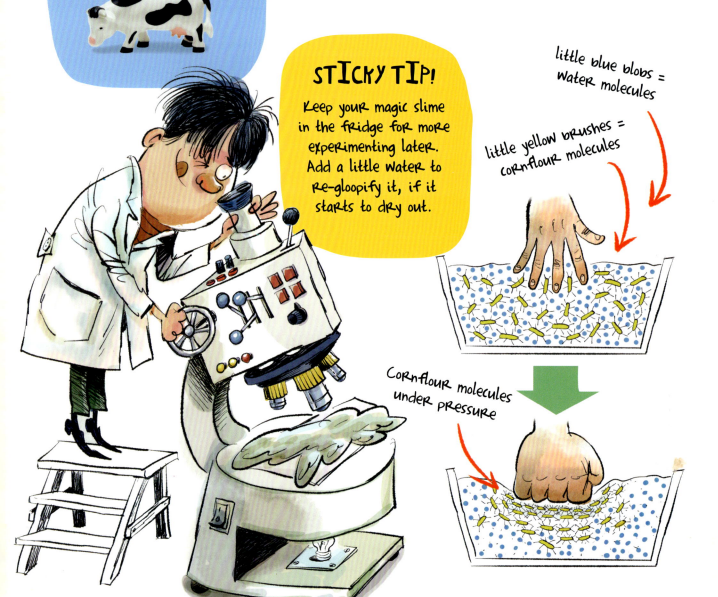

little blue blobs = water molecules

little yellow brushes = cornflour molecules

cornflour molecules under pressure

Quicksand

Quicksand acts a lot like oobleck. It forms when water wells up underground and soaks through loose soil or sand. Under normal conditions, the solid particles do not slide around much because of a force called friction. As water separates the particles, however, this force weakens. The weaker the friction gets, the more 'liquidy' the ground becomes.

The trick with quicksand is having just the right amount of water. If the ground is only a bit damp, the friction remains and the ground stays solid. If the ground becomes too wet, a puddle may form or the particles may flow away. But if the particles are just the right distance apart, the ground will continue to look solid – but it isn't. It is now 'quick'. Don't believe it? Step on it and see!

Centuries ago, scientist Isaac Newton (1642 - 1727) came up with rules to describe how liquids behave under pressure. Liquids that don't follow these rules are called non-Newtonian substances. Oobleck and quicksand are both part of this group.

Argh, I'm stuck!

Flubber Slime

Let's keep the slimy theme going! Unlike the last concoction you made, this slime doesn't change from one state to another. It just stays ooey, gooey and completely ICKY all the time. Are you okay with that? Yes, we thought you would be. Let's go!

WHAT YOU'LL NEED

- 120 ml PVA glue
- 1/2 tablespoon bicarbonate of soda
- food colouring
- 1/2 tablespoon contact lens solution
- mixing bowl
- stirring spoon

Making the flubber slime

1 Squeeze all of the PVA glue into the mixing bowl. Add the bicarbonate of soda. Stir well.

2 Add a few drops of food colouring (any colour you like). Stir to mix.

3 Add the contact lens solution. Stir to mix. Almost instantly the ingredients will congeal into a thick slime.

4 Now it's time to get messy! Plunge your hands right into the gloop and KNEAD, KNEAD, KNEAD. At first, the substance will be a little bit wet and gooey. As you knead, the moisture will mix in. Soon you will be holding a ball of smooth, silky slime. YUCK! Add a little more contact lens solution if your slime seems too wet.

EWW!

GROSS!

Play with your flubber slime

☀ Pull the slime apart. How far can you stretch it?

☀ Try cutting the slime with scissors. Does it work? It depends on how thick you've made your gloop!

☀ Use biscuit cutters to make shapes out of the slime. They won't last long – they'll melt into puddles of goo – but they're fun while they last.

☀ How does temperature affect your slime? Put some slime under a lamp until it is nice and warm. Put another blob of slime into your fridge. What differences do you notice?

The sticky, stinky science

There are three different substances at work in your flubber slime:

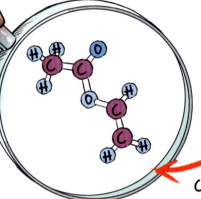

PVA glue is something scientists call a linear polymer. This means its molecules are long and stringy, like spaghetti strands.

Contact lens solution contains boric acid. This is related to a mineral called borax that dissolves easily in water.

Water (in the contact lens solution) contains hydrogen atoms, which like to link to other things.

When you combine glue, boric acid and water, the boric acid links with some of the water's hydrogen atoms to form ions, which are electrically charged particles. Because of their shape, these ions link with the glue's long molecules and sort of 'tie' them together to form a tangled polymer. Everything gets stuck together in a gloopy lump! The bicarbonate of soda makes it all a bit firmer, giving the perfect texture to your gooey slime.

STORE YOUR SLIME

When you're finished playing with your slime, store it in a resealable plastic bag. It should last for a couple of weeks.

SWAP IT

Just like contact lens solution, some laundry detergents contain boric acid. If you add a few drops of the right detergent to PVA glue, it will form slime too. Try it and see!

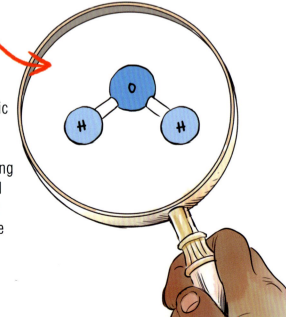

Hagfish: Champion of Slime

When it comes to making slime, the hagfish is the world champion! This eel-like fish grows up to 1.2 metres long. Its smooth skin is dotted with up to 200 'slime pores', which can blast out sticky mucus. The mucus forms a slimy coat around its body.

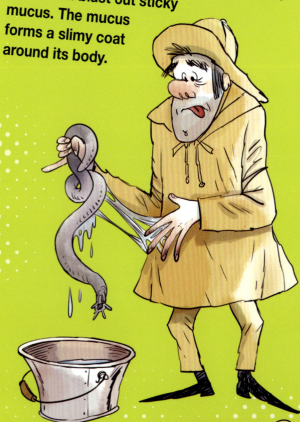

The hagfish mostly uses its slime for defence, squirting it out when it feels threatened. It probably doesn't need to do this very often, since other sea creatures know that hagfish slime is nasty, making it impossible to eat. Predators tend to leave the hagfish alone.

Another way a hagfish uses its slime is more practical and much, much more disgusting. To feed, it burrows into carcasses on the sea floor. The slime lubricates the hagfish and makes it easier for it to squirm around and tunnel inside the carcass whilst it eats. EUGH!

Rubber Egg

Takes 5 days

Challenge time! Can you remove the shell from a raw egg without getting your hands covered in sticky egg slime? You certainly can – if you know the trick. Here's how to do it.

WHAT YOU'LL NEED

- an egg (raw)
- glass jar or cup
- white vinegar
- running water

Removing the shell

1 Put the egg into the jar. Be careful not to crack it.

2 Pour white vinegar into the jar until the egg is completely covered.

3 Let the experiment sit for five days. Yes, FIVE DAYS!

4 Remove the egg and rinse it under running water. You should find that the shell has disappeared. Gently touch and squeeze it, holding it over the sink, just in case. It has turned into a rubber egg!

Take your experiment further

Your rubber egg is cool, but do you know what would be even cooler? A SUPER-SIZE rubber egg! Put your egg into a glass of water and let it sit overnight. In the morning, the egg will be much bigger. The egg sucks in water through its membrane to grow...GROW...GROW!

The sticky, stinky science

Vinegar is a type of acid. It reacts with the eggshell, which is made of a material called calcium carbonate. The reaction dissolves the eggshell but the vinegar does not react with the membrane underneath, so that part stays intact. The membrane is very thin and can break easily, so be careful!!!

Making an Egg

You have just un-made an eggshell. But how was it made in the first place? Egg production is an amazing and astonishingly fast process!

An egg begins when a chicken forms a yolk (the round yellow part) inside its body. Within about 15 minutes, the liquid yolk is encased in a membrane. About three hours later, the yolk is surrounded by sticky clear stuff – what we call the egg white.

Now comes the fun part! The gooey blob moves into an organ inside the chicken, called the shell gland. Here, calcium produced by the chicken surrounds the egg. It takes just 20 hours for the eggshell to form. When the process is complete, the chicken 'poops' out the egg. Yes, you heard that right – the egg comes out of the same hole as the poo. YUMMY! Who wants some breakfast?

Bendy Bones

Besides eggshells, what else is made of calcium? Hint: it's hard and is found inside you. Actually, there are over 200 of them in your body. That's right, we're talking about your BONES! What would happen if you put a bone into vinegar, like you did with the egg? There's only one way to find out…

Takes 1 week

Soak the bone

1 Save a chicken bone from your dinner – a thick one, like a drumstick, works best. Try to bend it. Hard, isn't it?

2 Wash the bone well to remove all the bits of food, then put it into the jar.

3 Pour white vinegar into the jar until the bone is completely submerged.

4 Let the experiment sit for one week.

5 Remove the bone and rinse it under running water. Try to bend it. If it doesn't bend, put it back into the vinegar and leave it for a few more days.

WHAT YOU'LL NEED

- a cooked chicken bone
- glass jar or cup
- white vinegar
- running water

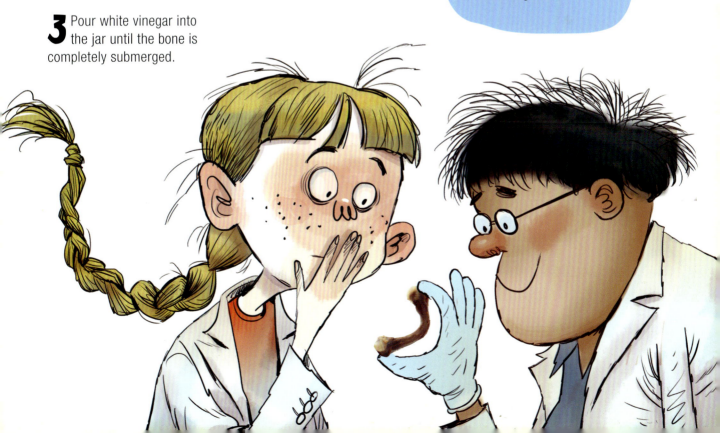

WOBBLY LEGS

The femur, or thigh bone, is the longest and strongest bone in the human body. Its length is about 1/4 of a person's height. It would take a LOOOOONG time to rubberise a femur! No reputable scientist will admit to having done this, but several have guessed that it would take a couple of months, at least.

The sticky, stinky science

Remember how vinegar dissolved the eggshell in the Rubber Egg experiment? It does the same thing to the calcium in the chicken bone. Calcium is the stuff that hardens bones. When it is gone, only squishy cartilage is left, which bends easily. YUCK!

Nose

Ear

Throat

Shoulder joint

Rib cage

Between spinal disks

Hip joint

Knee joint

These labels show the places where cartilage is common in the human body. Which can you feel?

Squishy Sharks

Land creatures, including people, need hard skeletons to support their weight. Ocean creatures are supported by water, so their skeletons can be more flexible – in the case of sharks, the skeletons are not hard at all! Sharks' skeletons are made entirely of cartilage. This is a strong but flexible tissue. A bendy skeleton lets a shark twist and turn in all sorts of ways to catch speedy prey.

In some parts of its body, like the skull and jaws, a shark does need some extra solidity. The cartilage is strengthened with calcium salts in these places. It still isn't bone, but it's harder than cartilage alone. A shark's teeth, of course, need to be really tough. They are coated with a hard layer of enamel that can slice through the flesh of their prey like a knife.

DID YOU KNOW?

Cartilage weighs much less than bone. Lighter skeletons help sharks to move quickly and easily through the water. That's part of the reason sharks are such super predators!

Lemon Volcano

This experiment is sticky AND smelly, in all the right ways. Your work area will be lemony-fresh when this vapour-iffic volcano erupts!

Make the lemon volcano

WHAT YOU'LL NEED

- lemon
- popsicle stick
- red food colouring
- washing-up liquid
- baking powder
- bowl
- adult helper

1 Ask your adult helper to slice off the top and bottom of the lemon and scoop out the insides to about halfway down. Put the lemon into the bowl with the hollow end facing upwards.

2 Poke the stick into the middle of the lemon. Use it to mash the lemon's insides and release lots of juice.

3 Squeeze a few drops of food colouring into the lemon.

4 Add a generous squeeze of washing-up liquid to the lemon.

5 Ready for some action? Here we go! Add a spoonful of baking powder. Right away, things will start to bubble and foam. Red 'lava' will rise to the top and begin to overflow.

6 To speed up your eruption, gently squeeze the sides of the lemon. KABOOM! Even more bubbles fizz into life. This experiment really has a lot of juice!

STINKY TIP!

The bigger the lemon, the longer the eruption. Use the biggest lemon you can find for this experiment.

The sticky, stinky science

Lemon juice is a type of acid. Baking powder is something called a base. When acids and bases come into contact with each other, a chemical reaction occurs. The reaction releases carbon dioxide gas.

In your Lemon Volcano experiment, the reaction occurs very quickly, so lots and lots of carbon dioxide gas is released at once.

The washing-up liquid traps the gas bubbles to create ooey, gooey, foamy 'lava'.

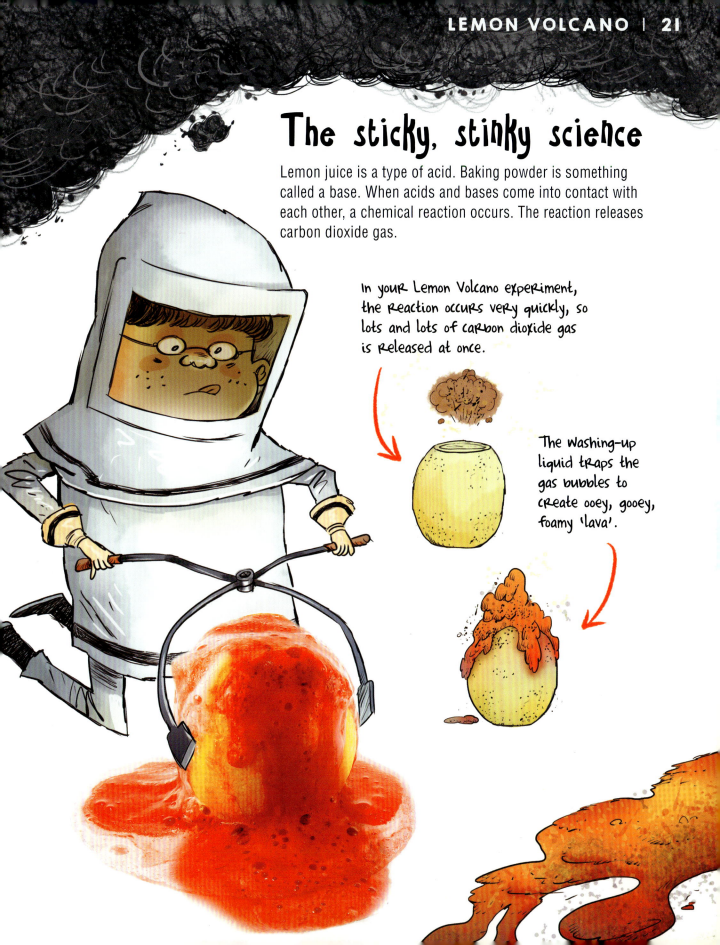

Take your experiment further

☀ Squeeze the juice from a second lemon into a cup. Add this to the volcano lemon, a few drops at a time. What happens?

☀ Other citrus fruits, such as oranges and grapefruit, are also acidic (although not as much as lemons). Do they make good volcanoes? Try it and see.

☀ Vinegar, cola, some fruit juices and pickle juice, are all acidic liquids. What happens if you put baking powder into them?

☀ Ask your adult to help you build a volcano out of soil in your garden. Put food colouring, washing-up liquid, vinegar or lemon juice, and baking powder into the volcano. See if you can make a big mess!

SOUR STUFF

Strong acids can damage human flesh, but there are plenty of acids, like the one found in lemon juice, that are weak enough for us to eat. Acids taste sour. Apart from lemons, can you think of other foods that taste sour? Do some research to find out if these foods are acidic.

vinegar

cola

See page 36 for the pH scale!

Stomach Acid

Your stomach is full of super-strong acid. The things you eat and drink plunge down your throat into this terrifying acid pool, where they start to dissolve. The muscles of the stomach squish and squeeze to churn everything around, like clothes in a washing machine.

BURP!

BURP!

If everything is working correctly, your stomach acid stays in your stomach. A mucus coating protects the stomach's inner walls, but sometimes a little bit of acid might splash up into your throat, where it can irritate the skin – ouch! This pain is called heartburn (although it has nothing to do with the heart; it's just in the same area).

MAKING BUBBLES

Want to see what happens inside your stomach? With an adult's permission, drop an antacid tablet into an acidic liquid. Watch the bubbles erupt!

To cure heartburn, people swallow pills called antacids. They're made of a chalky material similar to baking powder. Inside your tummy, the antacids react with the acid, neutralising it to stop the pain. In the process carbon dioxide is created, which has to escape from your body... can you guess how? You've got it – BURRRRRP!!!

Perfect Pennies

Grab a handful of coins and take a good look at them. What do you see? You probably see LOTS and LOTS of grime, and it's no wonder. Many coins have been making the rounds for decades. It's time they had a little bath, don't you think? Sadly for you, coin baths are STINKY… but they get the desired results. It's sparkle time!

WHAT YOU'LL NEED

- several coins (the dirtier, the better)
- 60 ml white vinegar
- 1 teaspoon salt
- stirring spoon
- non-metal bowl
- running water
- paper towel

Cleaning the coins

1 Put the vinegar and salt into the bowl. Stir until the salt dissolves.

2 Place the coins into the bowl. Push them around with the spoon to separate them. Arrange them so they don't overlap one another at all.

3 Let the coins sit for five minutes.

4 Use the spoon to flip the coins over. Let them sit for five more minutes.

5 Pour the coins into your hand over a sink. Rinse them under running water, then put them on a paper towel to dry. You'll see that the coins are now sparkling clean!

The sticky, stinky science

Lots of coins contain a metal called copper. Over time, copper reacts with oxygen in the air to form a dark, dull substance called copper oxide, also referred to as tarnish.

What about the vinegar and salt? You already know that vinegar is a stinky acid. Combined with salt, it gets SUPER ACID POWERS. These two substances together make hydrochloric acid, which is much stronger than vinegar acid alone. (Don't worry – it's still not strong enough to hurt you.) The hydrochloric acid reacts with the copper oxide, stripping it off the coin. BYE-BYE, TARNISH!

NOT JUST FOR BURGERS

Tomato sauce contains salt and vinegar. Could it clean a coin? Try it along with other acids you find, such as orange juice and cola. Which works best?

Dirty Money

Money really gets around. Coins and paper notes can circulate for decades, and they may change hands several times a day. Three or four people a day, times 365 days a year, times 20 years or so… that's a LOT of hands on your money. And that means a LOT of opportunities to pick up germs.

How dirty is money, really? Scientists have the answer! A study in 2014 grew bacterial cultures from paper notes and coins. The cultures contained 93 different strains of bacteria! Most of them were harmless to people, but they found a few – like the bacteria that causes pneumonia – that were pretty nasty.

So, what's to be done? Not much, unless you never want to touch money again, which is 1) not practical and 2) no fun at all. Experts say the best way to deal with the germs on money is to wash your hands frequently. And here's the big no-no: NEVER pay for food and then eat it without washing your hands in-between. Whatever that money is carrying, would go STRAIGHT into your mouth!

Growing Soap

What do you do when you're about to run out of soap? Well, if you use the right kind of soap, you could just microwave it to make it bigger. Eh?? Does that really work? Absolutely, and you're about to see it in action!

WHAT YOU'LL NEED

- bar of Ivory brand soap
- microwave-safe plate
- microwave
- adult helper

Cooking the soap

1 Put the bar of soap onto a microwave-safe plate and put it in the microwave.

2 Ask your adult helper to set the microwave to cook on HIGH for one minute. Push the START button.

3 Make sure you're watching through the window, because you're about to see something amazing. The soap expands rapidly, growing to five or six times its original size!

4 Let the soap sit for several minutes to cool down, then remove it from the microwave. Touch it… feel it… explore it. How has it changed from its original form?

If purchasing from Australia, try the website: dough.tools

The sticky, stinky science

Ivory soap is different from most other types of bar soap. When it is produced, the gooey soap 'batter' is whipped to fill it with tiny air bubbles. As the soap hardens, it traps all of these air bubbles along with the water vapour they contain.

Here's where the science magic happens! Microwaves work by heating up water vapour. When water vapour heats up, it expands rapidly, which means all those tiny air bubbles in the soap blow up like little balloons. The soap keeps growing until the vapour escapes or the microwave stops.

Ivory soap has tiny air bubbles containing water vapour.

HEAT

When heated, the water vapour expands and the soap gets bigger.

Pumice

A rock called pumice is similar to the Ivory soap you used in this experiment. Pumice forms when molten rock called lava comes into contact with water. The sudden temperature change makes the lava bubble, like a boiling liquid. Then the lava cools into a solid. The process happens so quickly that the bubbles do not escape. They are locked forever inside the rock.

As pumice is full of gas, it is actually lighter than water. It is the only rock that floats! During some volcanic eruptions, huge rafts of pumice form and drift off into the sea.

The biggest pumice raft ever observed covered an area greater than 26,000 square kilometres – that's even bigger than Wales. Discovered in 2012, it came from an underwater volcanic eruption near New Zealand.

VOLCANIC ROCK

Pumice is an igneous Rock. Igneous Rocks form as the result of volcanic activity. Other common igneous Rocks include basalt, granite and obsidian.

Lickable Glue

5 STARS

Have you ever licked an envelope? What about a stamp? If you have, you will know they are coated with a substance that turns into wet, sticky glue when you lick it. In this experiment, you'll create your own lickable glue that you can use to seal whatever you like. Best of all, YOU get to choose the flavour. Science has never been so scrumptious!

WHAT YOU'LL NEED

- 3 tablespoons white vinegar
- packet (7 g) unflavoured gelatin
- 1 teaspoon sugar
- 1 teaspoon liquid flavouring of your choice
- microwave-safe cup or bowl
- stirring spoon
- paintbrush
- paper
- adult helper

Making the lickable glue

1 Pour the vinegar into the microwave-safe container. Ask an adult helper to microwave it for 30 seconds, then remove the container from the microwave.

2 Add the gelatin, sugar and liquid flavouring to the vinegar. Stir until the gelatin and sugar dissolve. This may take a minute or more, so be patient and keep stirring.

3 Draw a sticker design onto the paper and cut it out.

4 Dip your paintbrush into the mixture. Paint the mixture in a very thin layer onto the back of your sticker design.

5 Let the liquid dry completely. You now have a strip of dry glue, just like those on envelopes and stamps.

6 To activate your glue, simply stick out your tongue. LICK IT and STICK IT!

The sticky, stinky science

Glue is surprisingly complicated stuff. Let's take a look at the science of how it works. The force that sticks two objects together is called adhesive force, or adhesion. We might refer to it as 'stickiness'. For glue to work it has to be able to stick to itself, as well as other objects. This quality is called cohesion, and it's an essential property of all glues.

So we have adhesion, we have cohesion, and then we have air – the third and final factor in glue-ability. Glues contain water, which evaporates into air. As the water disappears, the glue hardens, and its clinging power increases. Before long you have totally hard glue – and totally stuck objects. Success!

STORE YOUR GLUE

To store your lickable glue, pour it into a small jar with a screw-on lid. The glue will keep for several weeks in the fridge. If it hardens, just microwave it without the lid for a few seconds to melt it again.

STICKY TIP!

Liquid flavourings, such as almond, vanilla and orange, are available in the baking section of supermarkets.

NUMBER 1 SCIENTIST

Snacking on Stamps

Does stamp and envelope glue qualify as food? Turns out it does! Tests run by the Food and Drug Administration (FDA) show that postage stamps in the United States contain, on average, one tenth of a calorie per lick.

In Britain postal glue has a different recipe. An average-sized British stamp has 5.9 calories per lick. An unusually large one can have up to 14.5 calories. That's like eating one gummy sweet!

YUM!

In 1990, Australia was the first country to mass produce self-adhesive stamps, so no calories there. But could you gain weight from licking lots of stamps? Maybe! Consider the case of Dean Gould of Suffolk, England. In 1995, Gould managed to lick 450 stamps and stick them to envelopes within four minutes for a world record. At 5.9 calories each, that would work out to 2,655 calories, which is more than an average adult man eats in a day. Stamp glue for breakfast, lunch and dinner – DELICIOUS!

Colour-Changing Cabbage

POO, WHAT'S THAT STINK? It's the sweet, sweet scent of science in action! In this experiment, you get to whip up a batch of sublimely stinky cabbage juice that has some very unusual properties. Hold your nose, because it's about to get smelly in here!

WHAT YOU'LL NEED

- a head of red cabbage
- water
- saucepan
- knife
- sieve
- jug
- 6 small see-through cups
- household substances to test (see ideas on p34)
- adult helper

Preparing the cabbage

1 Ask your adult helper to chop the head of red cabbage into small pieces.

2 Put all of the cabbage into a saucepan. Add water until the cabbage is only just covered.

3 Ask your adult helper to heat the cabbage on a cooker until the water boils. Let the cabbage simmer for about 15 minutes, then remove it from the heat. Allow the mixture to cool completely.

4 Pour the cabbage juice (which should be a lovely shade of purple) through a sieve into a jug. You can throw away the cabbage – or eat it, if you like!

HYDROGEN SULPHIDE

Cooked cabbage stinks because the cooking process releases a gas called hydrogen sulphide. This is the same smell that wafts out of rotten eggs. Many people dislike eating cabbage because of this smell. Cabbage is really good for you though, so don't be afraid to give it a try!

The cabbage indicator

1 Put the six see-through cups on a flat surface. Pour a little bit of cabbage juice into each cup.

2 Look at the list of ideas for substances below. Choose six substances to test.

3 Now comes the fun part! Add a little bit of one substance into the first cup. Continue with your other chosen substances in the other cups. What do you see? It's pretty spectacular!

STINKY TIP!

To get rid of the cabbage smell, leave small bowls of vinegar sitting on your kitchen counter. It might take a few hours, or even overnight, but the vinegar will neutralise the odour.

SUBSTANCES TO TEST

lemon juice	fizzy drink
apple juice	shampoo
vinegar	laundry starch
milk	spit
window cleaner	baking soda
washing-up liquid	cola
mouthwash	orange juice

milk

baking soda

window cleaner

cola

The sticky, stinky science

Red cabbage juice is a natural indicator. This means it reacts to acids and bases by changing its colour. The juice starts out purple, but it instantly turns pink in the presence of acids and green in the presence of bases.

In the 'Substances to Test' list on page 34, some of the substances are acids and some are bases. You already know that lemon juice is an acid from previous experiments. Can you tell whether the other substances are acids or bases? And can you work out which are the strongest? Hint: the greater the colour change, the stronger the acid or base!

Take your experiment further

☀ Add any acid to a cup of cabbage juice until it changes colour. Now add a base to the same cup. What happens?

☀ Make indicator strips by soaking coffee filter paper in cabbage juice. Let the paper dry completely, then cut it into pieces. Put drops of different liquids on the strips to test them. Watch the colour change!

orange juice

vinegar

washing-up liquid

window cleaner

vinegar

lemon juice

The pH Scale

Acids and bases are measured by something called pH. This stands for 'potential of hydrogen', but don't worry too much about what that means; it's really complicated! All you need to know is that the pH scale goes from 0 to 14. A measurement of 7 is considered neutral. Anything higher than 7 is a base and anything lower than 7 is an acid. The further a measurement falls towards either end of the scale, the stronger the acid or the base.

⚠️

WARNING!

Strong acids and bases can both burn your skin. Don't touch either one!

Battery acid · Lemon · Tomato · Coffee · Rain Water · Milk · Tap Water · Egg · Liquid soap · Ammonia · Bleach · Drain cleaner

0 1 2 3 4 5 6 7 8 9 10 11 12 13 14

ACIDIC — NEUTRAL — BASIC

The chart above shows the pH scale with common substances found at each level. You can see that water and milk are right in the middle. Many foods are acidic and most cleaning products are basic. Where do you think your body sits on the scale? Do some research and find out!

Mould Garden

Mould is just generally nasty stuff. Some of it is stinky too. Would you like to grow some? OF COURSE you would! Luckily for you, this experiment keeps all the mould tucked away safely in sealed bags to keep the smell in. But you'll be able to see the mould perfectly well, in all its icky, sticky, hairy glory.

WHAT YOU'LL NEED

- 6 slices of bread
- water
- 6 see-through resealable plastic bags
- permanent marker

Growing the mould

1 Sprinkle a little water onto a slice of bread. You don't want the bread to be wet; just a teeny-tiny bit damp will do.

2 Wipe the damp side of the bread against any surface – a table, the floor, or even your own stinky armpit! Put the bread into a plastic bag and seal it.

3 Use a permanent marker to label the bag with what you wiped the bread on – the 'wipe site'.

4 Repeat steps 1 to 3, with the other five slices of bread, wiping each one against a different surface.

5 Put the bags in a warm place for a few days. Watch as your mould gardens erupt!

STINKY TIP!

This experiment works best and fastest with preservative-free bread. Ask an adult to help you find the right kind if you're not sure.

⚠️ WARNING!

Don't eat the bread after completing your samples! Throw it away once you've finished and wash your hands.

The sticky, stinky science

Mould is a microscopic organism from the fungi kingdom. It is related to mushrooms and yeast. Its 'seeds' are called spores, and they are EVERYWHERE. They're on your walls, your clothes, the roof of your car, the trees in your garden, your dog and even on YOU. Luckily, this is normal, and a few mould spores here and there won't do you any harm. Though it's important that you throw your experiment away at the end – it's not okay to eat mouldy bread!

When you rub bread against any surface, you pick up the spores. Closing the bread into plastic bags gives the mould a nice, warm, moist, protected home. It's just like planting a seed, except you're not growing pretty flowers. You're growing icky, hairy gunk. YUCK!

Mould comes in lots of different colours, so there's no telling what each mould garden will look like. You just have to wait and see!

Mouldy Cheese

Would you like a little mould with your dinner? You might think that's a ridiculous question... but think again! People all over the world adore a mouldy treat called blue cheese. The blue-green veins in this delicacy come from moulds called *Penicillium roqueforti* and *Penicillium glaucum*. These moulds are not harmful to people and they give the cheese a very distinctive and very popular flavour.

To make blue cheese, the appropriate mould spores are mixed with the cheese ingredients. The mixture is then 'needled', or punched full of small holes. These little holes let air into the ripening cheese and the air allows the mould spores to grow. The blossoming mould fills the air holes with stinky and delicious fuzz. BON APPÉTIT!

MEDICAL MOULD

Penicillium moulds do not only make delicious cheese. They are also used to make medicines called antibiotics that can kill harmful bacteria. Discovered in 1928, a Penicillium-based drug called penicillin was found to cure deadly illnesses. This revolutionised the field of medicine. It just goes to show that mould CAN be good for you!

Worm Farm

Earthworms are sticky and a little slimy too. That makes them the perfect pets, right? A simple worm farm will let you enjoy these creatures as they go about their wiggly, wriggly business.

WHAT YOU'LL NEED

- 6 to 10 live earthworms
- clean, empty 2-litre plastic bottle
- scissors
- small stones
- soil
- sand
- fruit and vegetable waste
- sticky tape
- plate
- adult helper

⚠️ WARNING!

Your sweat contains salt that is toxic to worms. Wear plastic gloves if you want to handle your slimy friends.

Making the farm

1 The first step is to find some worms! Worms like moist, dark places, so look under logs and leaves. You can also dig in loose, damp soil. If all else fails, you can buy live worms at many pet shops or places that sell fishing supplies.

2 Ask your adult helper to cut off the top of the plastic bottle.

3 Then ask your helper to make several small holes in the bottom of the bottle. These are for drainage.

4 Put small stones into the bottom of the bottle. The stone layer should be about 3 to 4 centimetres deep.

Ooh, a new home!

5 Add a 2-centimetre layer of soil and half of your worms. Cover the worms with another 2-centimetre layer of soil. The soil should be loose, not packed.

6 Add a 3-centimetre layer of sand on top.

7 Repeat steps 5 and 6 to add another soil–worm–soil–sand layer.

8 Drop some fruit and vegetable waste (such as peelings) onto the top layer.

9 Use sticky tape to attach the cut-off bottle top onto the top of your worm farm.

10 Put the whole thing on a plate (in case water drips out of the drainage holes). Then put your farm in a warm, dark place such as in a cupboard, or wrap thick paper around you worm farm to block out light.

Takes 2 weeks

HOME SWEET HOME

Top tips for looking after your worms

✳ Check on your worms every day to see what they are doing. You should be able to see the trails and burrows made by the worms as they mix the materials together.

✳ Make sure your worm farm is in a dark and warm place. This is VERY IMPORTANT for the happiness of your worms: they hate light and cold.

✳ Worms also need dampness to stay healthy. Add a small amount of water to your worm farm every day.

✳ Occasionally add a little bit of food to keep your worms fed – do this whenever you see that their food supply is running low. Your worm farm will soon be in full swing!

The sticky, stinky science

Earthworms are mini soil factories. They eat rotting organic matter as they move around in the ground, then digest it and poo out the remains as beautiful, fertile soil.

Earthworms also churn the soil as they move underground, allowing air and water to get through. This helps plants by letting water reach their roots, and by making space for the roots to grow. Worm tunnels also bring air to underground animals and improve the soil's drainage. With all these benefits, worms are a vital part of any healthy environment.

Dinner's ready!

Worm Poo for Sale!

Worm poo, also called vermicompost, is thick, damp and almost black. It contains all sorts of digested organic matter. The worm's body breaks this matter down, so it's no longer rotting and is ready to return to the soil.

Why would you want to add worm poo to your soil? Because it's full of nutrients that plants just LOVE! Farmers spread the stuff on their fields by the truckload. Vermicompost helps seeds to grow into big, beautiful, healthy crops.

Farmers get their vermicompost from commercial worm farms. These businesses keep millions of worms in huge bins. Workers add rotting organic matter to the bins every day and the worms do their thing. The resulting 'black gold', as it is sometimes called, is scraped from the bottoms of the bins, then bagged and sold. Thanks, worms!

WORM SPEED

On a worm farm, it takes about two months for worms to turn a fresh batch of food into vermicompost. Worms eat about half their own body weight each day!

Dissolving Cucumbers

Fresh cucumbers are crunchy and delicious. Under the right (or should we say wrong?) circumstances however, they dissolve into sticky, slimy goo. Do you want to see this happen? Of course you do! Just follow the instructions.

Takes 5 days

Preparing the cucumber

WHAT YOU'LL NEED

- a cucumber
- 1 teaspoon of water
- resealable plastic bag
- knife
- cutting board
- adult helper

1 Roll the cucumber back and forth on a flat surface, like a rolling pin. Press down hard on it as you do. You could even bang it on the table a little bit. Your aim is to bruise it.

2 Ask an adult helper to chop the cucumber into slices. Let the slices sit in the open air for about 10 minutes.

3 Put the slices into a resealable plastic bag. Add one teaspoon of water.

4 Seal the bag, then shake it to get the cucumber pieces nice and wet.

5 Put the bag in a warm place, such as near a lamp that gives off heat. Let it sit for four to five days. Check the bag every day. What do you see?

CHECK IT OUT

Freeze a few cucumber slices, then let them thaw. The freezing process damages the cucumber's tissues. The result is pretty slimy!

The sticky, stinky science

It won't take long for the cucumber pieces to start dissolving into slime! This process begins when you bruise and cut the cucumber. Airborne bacteria enter the cucumber in the damaged places. Cucumber-eating bacteria love damp conditions, so they thrive inside the wet, sealed bag. They multiply… and as they do, they eat the cucumber, which decomposes into a slimy mess. Disgusting!

Eugh, this is gross!

THROW IT AWAY

Throw your cucumber slime into the bin or compost when you've finished looking at it. It's not ok to eat it! YUCK!

From Farm to Shop

As they bruise so easily, cucumbers are difficult to transport. They have to be handled very gently, almost like eggs, all the way from the field to the shop.

Science has stepped in to make the process easier. Cucumbers with thicker, tougher skins have been developed and are often sold in supermarkets, because they are so convenient. However, they're not the only option! There are well over 100 cucumber varieties.

Some people say the supermarket types are bland and tasteless compared to others, and recommend buying cucumbers from a farmers' market instead, for better taste and texture. Farmers transport their thin-skinned cucumbers very carefully to market, offering you a bruiseless and bacteria-free cucumber for a delicious meal.

DID YOU KNOW?

Most people think cucumbers are vegetables, but they're not! They are actually a type of berry. By weight, they are 95 per cent water.

Spoilt Milk

Have you ever taken a big gulp of creamy, delicious milk… only to discover that it's gone bad? EUGH! Spoilt milk not only tastes disgusting, it can also go chunky and it smells HORRIBLE. Do you want to see and smell it for yourself? No? Go on, it's for science.

YUCK! Don't drink these!

Spoiling the milk

1 Use the permanent marker to label the cups: 1, 2 and 3.

2 Pour an equal amount of milk into each cup. About 2 centimetres should do the trick.

3 Put the cups in different places around your house. Choose places with different conditions – for instance, a warm spot, a cool spot, an outdoor spot, a damp spot, etc.

4 Check on the cups once a day. In your notebook, write down what you see and smell. Use the cup numbers to correctly keep track of your observations.

5 After three or four days, the milk in at least one of your cups should have turned solid and stinky. REALLY stinky. Take a big sniff – then throw it away, because it'll stink out your whole house!

6 Keep checking the other cups until they reek too. This is the sweet, sweet stench of science success! Which condition kept the milk fresh for the longest?

Takes 1 week

Friendly bacteria

WHAT'S SO GREAT ABOUT SKIMMED?

Fat helps to preserve milk. Skimmed milk contains very little fat, so it turns sour faster than semi-skimmed or full-fat milk.

The sticky, stinky science

All milk contains bacteria. During processing, the milk is treated to remove germs that cause illness, but some 'friendly' ones are left in there. Over time, these bacteria change proteins in the milk into a chemical called ammonia. Ammonia is – you guessed it – really stinky! That's why spoilt milk smells so bad. Don't drink it!

The solid 'chunking' effect takes place due to a process called curdling, where tiny solid bits in the milk separate from the liquid. All of these changes happen more quickly in warmer conditions. That's why it is always good to keep your milk in the fridge!

Read the Label

You might have noticed dates printed on packaged food from the supermarket, including on milk. What do these dates mean?

SELL BY: Food isn't supposed to be sold after the 'sell by' date. It's still good, though, with about 30 per cent of its life left after this date. It's fine for you to buy it on the last day and use it for a while longer.

BEST BEFORE: A 'best before' date means the food will be tastiest up until a certain time. After that, it may still be edible, but it may not taste quite as good.

USE BY: The 'use by' date means business. You should consume the food by this date. After that, it might look and smell fine, but that's no guarantee it is safe – dangerous bacteria could be lurking inside. Do yourself a favour and bin it!

⚠️ WARNING!

Eating food past the 'use by' date can lead to food poisoning. This probably won't kill you, but it can make you really ill. You don't want this to happen – trust us!

1309 7862 07 M1
UK-7-174M
DISPLAY UNTIL
18 JAN
BEST BEFORE
24 JAN

Fart Detective

Takes 2 weeks

Hold onto your bottom, because it's about to get smelly in here. We're going to venture into the unmentionable realm of FARTS – those sneaky, smelly, embarrassing emissions that we all deny, but we all produce. It's true! Your mum farts, your teachers fart, your favourite film stars fart, kings and queens fart… and YOU fart. Yes, YOU! And this experiment will prove it!

WHAT YOU'LL NEED

- notebook
- pen or pencil
- various farty foods

FARTY FOODS

The foods on this list are notorious fart producers. Pick one and give it a go!

- beans (all types)
- dairy products (milk, cheese, ice cream)
- whole grains (wheat, oats)
- vegetables (Brussels sprouts, cabbage, onions, broccoli, cauliflower)
- fizzy drinks (all types)
- fruit (apples, peaches, pears, grapes, prunes)

BAARRRP!

Track your trumps

1 First thing in the morning, write the date at the top of a page in your notebook. Keep the notebook somewhere you can reach easily as you go about your day.

2 All day long, each time you let one rip, whip out the notebook. Note the time and make notes about the fart's smell, power, or anything else you observe.

3 At the end of the day, count how many gassy episodes you recorded. Write the total at the bottom of the page.

4 Repeat steps 1 to 3 each day for a week. By this point, you'll have a really good idea of your trumping habits.

5 Now the experimentation begins! Choose a food from the list of ideas. Eat a generous serving of that food with your breakfast. It's okay if it isn't a breakfast food – it's for science.

6 Track your airy emissions during the day. Do you notice anything different, like more frequent or smellier gas? If so, write it down.

7 Repeat steps 5 and 6 every day with a new food. Continue experimenting for as long as you like. The fun could go on for months, particularly if you're a dedicated scientist! Your friends and family might not be so keen though.

DID YOU KNOW?

According to people who are interested in this kind of thing, humans fart at an average of 14 times a day. Are you an over achiever or an under producer? Inquiring minds want to know!

so gross!

The sticky, stinky science

The proper word for farts is 'flatulence'. There's nothing mysterious here – it's just gas that builds up in your intestines. Some of the gas is air that you swallow by accident whilst eating and drinking, and some of it is produced by bacteria. Gut bacteria break down the things you eat and drink, giving off gas in the process. This bacterial gas contains smelly chemicals – and that's why farts stink!

But why do some foods make you fart more? One reason is the amount of time it takes to digest the food – the longer the process, the greater the gas. Beans and other high-fibre foods take a long time for your body to break down, so voila! Farts. Another factor is food sensitivities. Anything you have trouble digesting will produce more gas. This can be different for each person – it's your very own fart profile!

BAARRRP!

That stinks!

DAY 1

	SMELL	POWER	NOTES
8:32	No smell	2/10	
8:45	Deadly	7/10	Silent!
9:30	Almost deadly	6/10	
10:15	Not bad	3/10	
11:43	No smell	1/10	Little
1:18	Slight smell	6/10	
3:50	Really smelly	10/10	LOUD
3:52	Lingering!	5/10	
6:00	No smell	4/10	At dinner

TOTAL: 9

PARP!

PARP!

What's That Sound?

PARP!

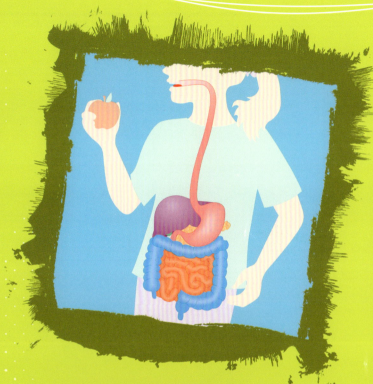

So now you know how farts are produced... but WHY, oh WHY, do they make that embarrassing noise? Well, let's find out.

To exit your intestines, gas passes into an area called the rectum. Then it has to leave the body through a little hole called the anus (the same hole your poo comes out of). As the gas passes through the anus, it sometimes makes the skin and muscles vibrate. This vibration creates sound waves and we hear that lovely BRRRRAAAAAP noise!

Or... not. Sometimes farts sneak out without making any sound at all. It really depends on the amount and speed of the gas being passed. A little gas at low speed = YOU'VE GOT AWAY WITH IT. Lots of gas at high speed = WAKE THE NEIGHBOURS. Whoopsie!

YOU HAVE BEEN WARNED!

The main causes of swallowing air are: eating too fast, drinking fizzy drinks, chewing gum and sucking on hard sweets. If you do any of these things, prepare to accept the stinky consequences!

BRRRRR AAAAP!

Scent Detector

When you smell something, either good or bad, what's really going on? This experiment will help you find out. Get a WHIFF of this one!

WHAT YOU'LL NEED

- 1 teaspoon of perfume
- food container with lid
- tape measure
- stopwatch or other timer
- notebook
- pen or pencil
- several friends or family members

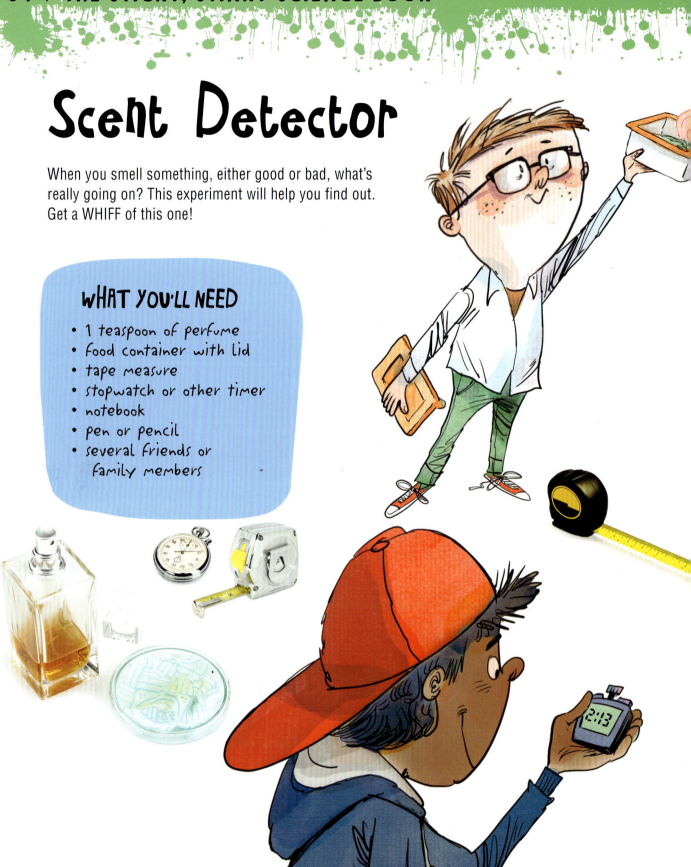

Getting smelly!

1 Pour a little perfume into a food container. Snap on the lid.

2 Take the container to a different room indoors. (You can't use the one you were just in, because it reeks of perfume now.) Put the container in one corner of the room.

3 Use a tape measure to find a distance of 3 metres from the container. Get a friend to stand at that spot. Ask the friend to tell you when they can smell something.

4 Open the container and immediately start your stopwatch or timer.

5 Stop the timer as soon as your friend reports a smell. Write down the time in your notebook.

6 Divide the number of seconds by 3 to find out how fast the scent travelled. For instance, if the friend smelled the perfume after 21 seconds, then 21 divided by 3 = 7 seconds per metre.

STINKY TIP!

Ask an adult first, and use the cheap stuff for this experiment! Don't waste your mum's good perfume!

SMELLING SPEED

Repeat the experiment with several other people. Use a different room for each test so your subjects won't pick up the smell from the last test. What do you notice? Why do you think there are differences in test times?

The sticky, stinky science

You know about molecules – the itty bitty particles that make up everything? Some substances cling tightly to their molecules. Others, not so much – their molecules constantly escape into the air, where they drift around. Sometimes they drift into a human nose. When they do, they hit olfactory (scent) receptors in the upper back of the nose and bind to them. The receptors 'read' the molecules to find out what they are. Then they shoot off a message to the brain. Your brain informs you that you're smelling baked bread, or garlic, or flowers, or dog poo, or whatever gave off those molecules.

THInk ABOUT IT

It's unlikely that all of the times for your experiment tests will be exactly the same. For one thing, some people have a better sense of smell than others. You can't control that. But your test location has an effect, too. What might account for any differences you notice? Here are a few suggestions:
• ceiling height of the room
• windows open or shut
• room temperature
• types of furniture/curtains/carpet.
Can you think of any others?

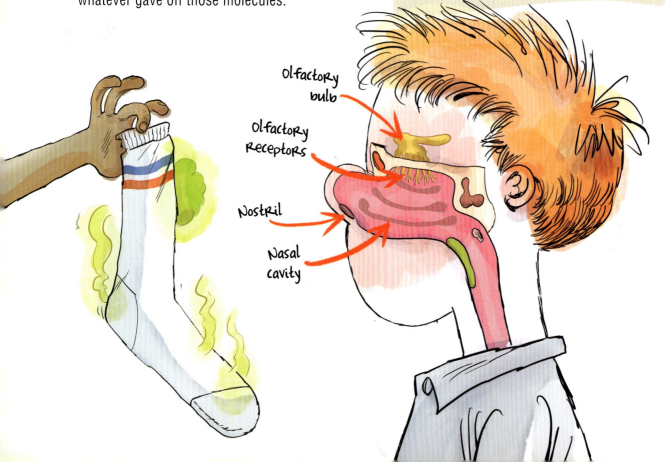

Olfactory bulb

Olfactory Receptors

Nostril

Nasal cavity

Stinky Skunks

Skunks are the stink champions of the animal world. These black and white bad boys have glands in their rear end that produce a sulphur-loaded liquid. Sulphur smells AWFUL. When the skunk lets loose... let's just say you're going to notice. A LOT. For a LONG TIME.

It wouldn't be so bad if the scent just drifted gently off the skunk's bottom. You could probably outrun that. But noooo! To deliver its disgusting blast, a skunk actually lifts its tail, aims its bottom and FIRES the smelly liquid at its intended target. Skunks are deadly accurate to about 3 metres, and pretty good at double that distance. So, if you're anywhere close to a skunk, you will probably get doused.

If this disaster happens to you (or perhaps your curious dog), a bath of baking powder and hydrogen peroxide will take away the stench. But really, who wants to do that? It's better to avoid skunks and call it a day!

DID YOU KNOW?

The smelly stuff in a skunk's spray is called a thiol. A thiol is a type of sulphur that is bonded to hydrogen and carbon. Sulphur gives the thiol a strong and particularly unpleasant odour. Lots of stinky things contain thiols, but the one skunks make smells especially horrible!

Mummified Fish

Takes 2-3 weeks

It's time for the grand finale of our sticky, stinky journey – this experiment is a little different. Instead of creating something nasty, you're going to take a yucky dead fish and DE-ickify it. That's right, you're going to MUMMIFY that creature. Read on to learn this time-tested method!

WHAT YOU'LL NEED

- plastic gloves
- bicarbonate of soda (2 kg)
- a 'dressed' fish, about 12 to 15 cm long
- container large enough to hold the fish
- plate

STICKY TIP!

Before you do anything else, put on the plastic gloves. You're going to be handling a dead fish.

Mummifying the fish

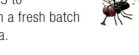

1 Put the bicarbonate of soda into the container to a depth of about 3 centimetres.

2 Lay the fish on its side in the container. Open up the fish, and pack the inside of the body with bicarbonate of soda.

3 Add more bicarbonate of soda on top until the fish is buried about 3 centimetres deep.

4 Now the wait begins! Leave the container undisturbed (and uncovered) for one week in a dry area.

5 Remove the fish and tip out all of the bicarbonate of soda. Brush any powder off the fish, inside and out.

6 Follow steps 1 to 3 to re-pack the fish in a fresh batch of bicarbonate of soda.

7 Now we wait AGAIN (sorry). Let the container sit for another week to ten days.

8 Put on those gloves yet again. Remove the fish from the bicarbonate of soda and brush off all the powder.

9 The moment you've been waiting for has finally arrived! At this point the fish should be totally dried out. Put your shrivelled fish on a plate and examine it to your heart's content. You have created your very own mummy!

DRESSED FISH

A 'dressed' fish isn't wearing a dinner jacket. This word means it has been cleaned, and its guts have been removed. You can buy a small dressed fish very inexpensively at a supermarket.

The sticky, stinky science

Bicarbonate of soda has almost magical absorbing abilities. Due to the way its molecules are structured, it can suck up a great deal of water without getting soggy itself. The moisture in the fish escapes into the bicarbonate of soda, which causes the fish to dehydrate (that's the fancy scientific term for losing water).

But why doesn't the fish decay? Two reasons. First of all, rot-inducing bacteria and fungi need water to function. The dehydration process thwarts them. Mwahahaha! Secondly, the layer of bicarbonate of soda blocks new bacteria and fungi from getting to the fish corpse. As a result of these two factors, decay never sets in. You end up with a hard, dry, stinkless fish that is sort of disgusting… but incredibly cool!

Human Mummies

The ancient Egyptians are famous for their mummy-making abilities. They thought people needed their bodies in the afterlife, so they dehydrated the corpses of important people. It was a sign of great respect to be mummified!

The mummification process was similar to what you just did with your fish. First, the internal organs of the corpse were removed. Then all the body cavities were packed with a powder called 'natron', a salt found along the banks of the River Nile. Next, the body was fully packed in natron and allowed to sit for 70 days. When the drying process was complete, the body was cleaned off, stuffed with linen and sand to give it some shape, then wrapped in bandages. TA-DA! A mummy!

The process was so effective that the mummies could last for thousands of years. Many of them have survived to the present day.

HOW OLD?

The oldest known human mummies are nearly 7000 years old. Will your fish last that long? Wait and see!

Science Resources

Ok, it's safe to let go of your nose now. And you should also probably wash your hands. Your sticky, stinky journey is over... but the fun doesn't have to stop here! There is no end to the yucky science you can explore. Do some research in a library or online. Find more experiments to try, then go for it! When it comes to science, there's always a new mess waiting just around the corner...

Here are some great websites for you to explore. Some of the science is messy, some is clean, but it's all fascinating!

www.australiangeographic.com.au/experiments
Lot of experiments that can be done using things found around your home.

www.teacherstryscience.org
These teacher-approved science activities are educational and entertaining.

www.exploratorium.edu
Explore the fascinating ins and outs of science, art and human perception on this site.

www.billnye.com
The website of this popular scientist is packed with information and activities.

www.sciencenewsforstudents.org
What's the latest and greatest in the science world? Find out on this awesome news site.

science.howstuffworks.com
Did you ever wonder how things work? Here's the place to find out!

⚠ INTERNET SAFETY

Children should be supervised when using the internet, particularly when using an unfamiliar website for the first time. Publisher and author cannot be held responsible for the content of the websites referred to in this book.

Science Lingo

ACID
A chemical substance that often tastes sour, such as lemon juice. Strong acids can dissolve metal.

ATOM
Tiny particles that make up all matter.

BACTERIA
Microscopic single-celled organisms. Some bacteria can be helpful to people (by aiding digestion and other bodily processes), but some can be harmful (by causing disease).

BASE
A chemical substance that typically has a slippery texture, such as liquid soap.

DECOMPOSE
To disintegrate or decay an object down to the chemical elements it contains.

DEHYDRATION
The process of removing water from a substance or object.

FRICTION
Resistance created when objects rub or move against each other.

FUNGI
Organisms such as mould and yeast that survive by decomposing organic matter and then absorbing the nutrients it contains.

INDICATOR
A substance that changes colour in the presence of an acid or a base.

MICROSCOPIC
Too small to be seen without the help of a microscope.

MINERAL
A naturally occuring solid substance that is not an animal or a plant.

MOLECULE
A group of atoms bonded together that make up the smallest unit of a chemical compound.

ORGANIC
Something that contains the element carbon. All known life contains organic compounds.

POLYMER
A large molecule that has chains or rings of linked units.

REACTION
A chemical change that occurs when two substances come into contact with each other.

RECEPTOR
An organ or cell that can respond something, such as light, heat or scent, and send a signal to a sensory nerve.

SPORE
The reproductive body (similar to a seed) of certain organisms, such as mould.

WATER VAPOUR
The invisible gas form of water.

Index